For Molly: Space is for everyone
and especially for you.

—M. R. K.

For my ever-supportive
Mum and Dad.

—D. M.

Published by Roaring Brook Press
Roaring Brook Press is a division of Holtzbrinck Publishing Holdings Limited Partnership
120 Broadway, New York, NY 10271 · mackids.com

Text copyright © 2022 by Mary Robinette Kowal
Illustrations copyright © 2022 by Diana Mayo

Library of Congress Cataloging-in-Publication Data is available.
ISBN 978-1-250-25961-5

Our books may be purchased in bulk for promotional, educational, or business use.
Please contact your local bookseller or the Macmillan Corporate and Premium Sales Department
at (800) 221-7945 ext. 5442 or by email at MacmillanSpecialMarkets@macmillan.com.

First edition, 2022

ABOUT THIS BOOK
The illustrations for this book were handcrafted using acrylic paints,
colored pencils, pastels, and collaged elements, all tidied up with a little digital magic.
The text was set in Bachenas and Crayon Crumble and the display type is Providence and Carre Noir.
The book was edited by Connie Hsu and designed by Ashley Caswell with art direction by Jen Keenan.
The production was supervised by Susan Doran, and the production editor was Avia Perez.
Printed in China by Hung Hing Off-set Printing Co. Ltd., Heshan City, Guangdong Province

1 3 5 7 9 10 8 6 4 2

MOLLY
ON THE
MOON

Written by **MARY ROBINETTE KOWAL**
Illustrated by **DIANA MAYO**

ROARING BROOK PRESS
New York

Molly moved to the Moon.

She moved to the Moon to an underground room, and
rode on a rocket with her mom and her baby brother, Luke.

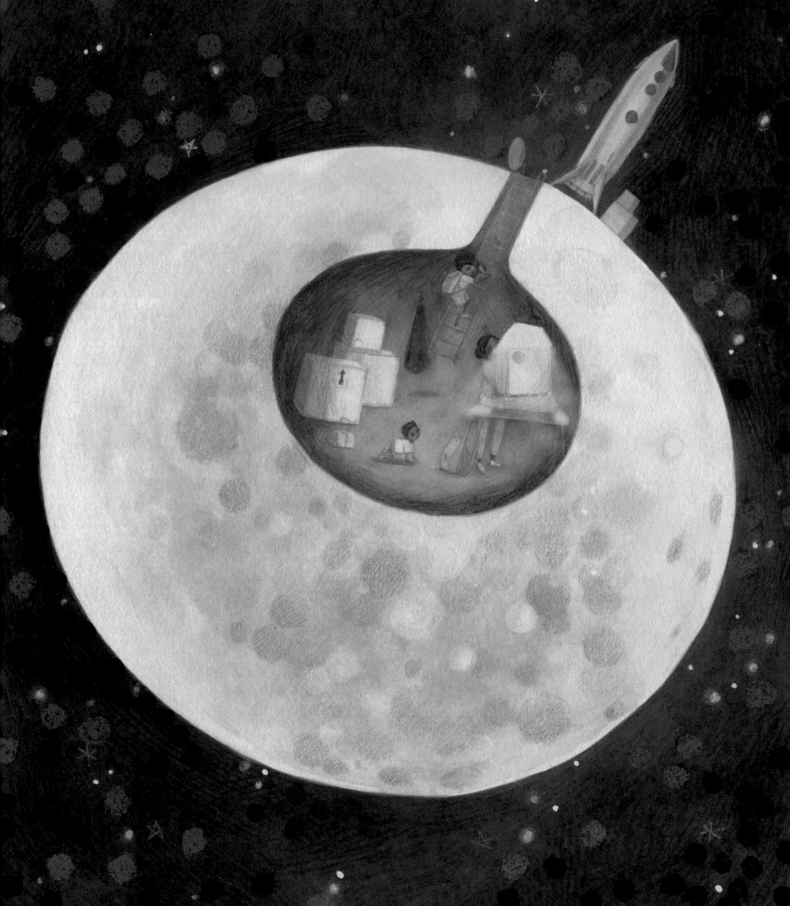

The room was called a module.
It wasn't very big, so Molly could bring
only one toy—her little lamb, Lassie.

But there were the packing
crates that the food came in.

Those became a fort.

The fort and Lassie were her only toys on the Moon . . .

except for the old solar panel cover.

That became a witch's cape!

But the fort and the witch's cape and
Lassie were her only toys on the Moon . . .

except for the tin cans.

Those became a tea set!

But the fort and the witch's cape and the tea set and Lassie were her only toys on the Moon.

One day, she went to get Lassie so that they could have tea in the fort together. But Lassie wasn't there.

Molly remembered that the Moon is a funny place where things weigh less.

On the Moon, very light things could get
pulled into the fan. But Lassie wasn't there either.

Then Molly heard a
noise inside her fort.

"Bababa!"

Inside Molly's fort, Luke was having
a tea party with her only toy.

"Hey! Lassie is mine."

Luke said, "BABABA!" and
clutched the lamb tighter.

"GIVE HER BACK!"

The gravity on the Moon is weaker than on
Earth, which made Molly seem extra strong.
And like Moon cookies, Luke seemed extra light,
like he didn't weigh much more than a feather pillow.

So when Molly pulled Lassie . . .

. . . she pulled Luke right over her head!
He let go of Lassie but kept going.

He landed on top
of the table and
bounced back
into the air.

He bounced off the bed and flew higher.

Molly reached for him, but Luke bounced
off her fingers and went even higher.

Their mother came in and snatched him out of the air. "Molly! What did we say about tossing the baby?"

"He took Lassie!"

"You have to be gentle, especially on the Moon."

It wasn't fair. So Molly took her witch's cape
and Lassie and went into the fort.

Molly didn't even want tea anymore. She just wanted to sit and be mad.

"Ouch!" She'd sat on one of Luke's blocks, and that made her madder.

She started to throw the block
out of her fort but then stopped.
Molly looked at the block
and realized . . .

Luke had only blocks to
play with. He didn't have a
fort or a witch's cape or a tea set.
She had a stuffed animal
brought all the way from Earth.

He didn't have
anybody at all to play
with on the Moon.

Except for her.

Molly went to find her mother.

"Mama? Will you help me
sew something?"

The witch's cape was so light that the fan wanted to pull it up
to the ceiling. They had to pin it to the bed in order to cut it.

First, Molly cut out a rectangle-ish thing.

Then a roundish thing.

Then some tube things.

She sewed them all together into something
that might have been a lamb or it might have been a
dog or it might have been a hippopotamus.

When she gave it to Luke, he grabbed it.

"Bababa!" He jumped for joy.

Molly grabbed her little brother
before he could float too high . . .
and invited him to tea.

Molly lived on the Moon.

Molly lived on the Moon in an underground room
and had tea in her fort with Lassie and Bababa
and her baby brother, Luke.

AUTHOR'S NOTE

Do you wonder what it would be like to live on the Moon like Molly? It would be very different from life on Earth.

When you look at the Moon from Earth, the part that is bright is where it's daylight. The daylight part sloooowly changes over the course of a month. This means that for Molly, a day lasts half a month, and a night lasts half a month. The next time you see the real Moon, can you tell if it would be daytime or nighttime for her?

Those long days and nights are part of why Molly and her mom and her little brother, Luke, live in an underground room. The very long day means that the temperature on the surface heats up to about 250 degrees Fahrenheit, and the very long night makes it around –250 degrees Fahrenheit. Also, there's no air on the Moon! Living underground is the easiest way to be safe.

Another difference about living on the Moon is the gravity. Gravity is the force that makes things fall. The Moon's gravity is only one-sixth of our gravity. Imagine that you have six cookies on the Moon. (Mmm . . . cookies.) In one-sixth gravity, they would weigh as much as only one cookie on Earth. You can try asking your parents for cookies for this experiment, but I don't promise that they'll give them to you . . .

To understand a little more about how gravity works on the Moon, remember the buttons in the pictures. On the Moon, a button weighs about as much as a small feather on Earth. Get a feather and a button and drop them at the same time. On the Moon, the button will fall like the feather does here. Neat, right? Now see if you can keep the feather in the air like one of Molly's buttons on the Moon.

Gravity is part of why it is expensive to get to the Moon. It takes a lot of effort to lift something off Earth, and the heavier it is, the more effort it needs. That's why the module where Molly lives is so small and part of why Molly could take only one toy. If you were going to live on the Moon, what toy would you take?

Now . . . you've got one toy, plus so many more things you can play with. Can you make a fort from pillows? Or a cape from a blanket? What else can you make just from things around the house? Remember, if you're like Molly, you can't cut or break anything that still has to be used for its original purpose. (Check with your grown-up to be sure.) I bet you can make a lot of fun from ordinary items around the house and pretend you're on the Moon, too.

And when you finish, you can look up at the Moon and show Molly what you've made. Can you picture where she is? I bet she's waving back at you.

Oh! And remember, when you live on the Moon, it's very important not to toss the baby.

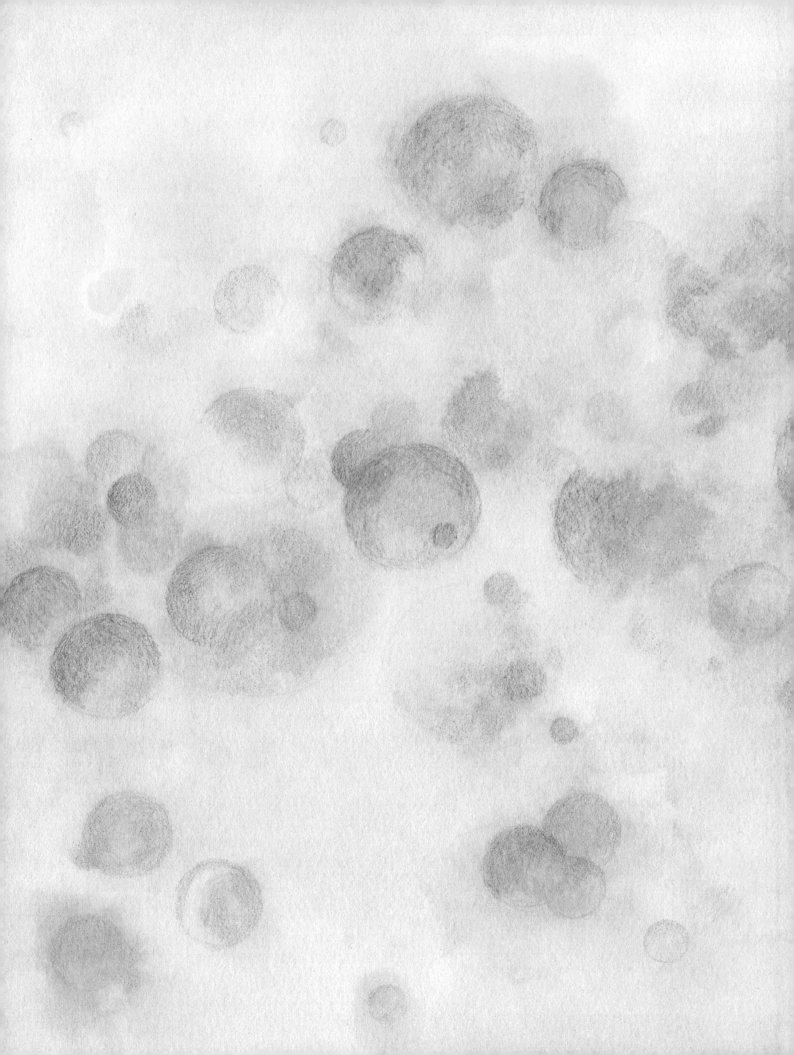